The Christmas Promise

A Victorian Christmas Novella

Gabrielle Meyer

Belle May Press

www.GabrielleMeyer.com

For Belle & May

Contents

Chapter One

Anglesey Abbey
Cambridgeshire, England
December 21, 1899

J ust five days. That was all Lady Ashleigh
Arrington must endure before this horrid affair
would be over. She stood in the echoing foyer,
forcing herself to offer their first houseguest a warm
smile and a curtsey. "Welcome to Anglesey Abbey,
Lady Houghton." Ashleigh's voice didn't quiver as
much as she had feared. "I hope you'll enjoy your
stay."

"I doubt it." Lady Houghton's lips pinched in
a distasteful expression as she clutched her small
poodle in one hand and a cane in the other. "My
rheumatism is acting up with this cold weather
and the rich holiday food doesn't agree with my
stomach. Rice and milk in the morning is all I can
tolerate."

"Of course. I'll speak to our cook personally."

The older lady studied Ashleigh with a critical
eye. "I do so hope you'll bring pride to your mother's

memory this week. You have a lot to live up to, young lady."

Ashleigh didn't let her smile falter, though inside she cringed. This would be the first Christmas they would celebrate since her mother had passed and it would be the most important. If Ashleigh didn't entertain her guests the way they were accustomed, the *London Examiner* would declare her a failure throughout England. More importantly, Anglesey Abbey would come to shame. She could not let that happen, for her father's sake.

"Lady Ashleigh will be a charming hostess." Father stood beside Ashleigh in a crisp black suit, his back straight and his confidence in Ashleigh evident for all to see. "She learned everything she knows from her mother."

Again, Ashleigh wanted to cringe. All around her, the large home spoke of elegance, refinement, and sophistication. None of which Ashleigh possessed, despite her mother's patient instructions. For generations, the mistresses of Anglesey Abbey had brought pride to the grand old manor house. Ashleigh suspected she would be the first in a long line to fail.

"Please allow Beatrice to show you to your room." Ashleigh nodded at one of the servants standing by to assist their guests.

At least a dozen maids and footmen stood at attention in a straight line along the edge of the echoing foyer. Their starched white aprons and tall collars gleamed within the dim interior.

"I hope you've given me one of the east-facing rooms," Lady Houghton said with a frown, as if Ashleigh had already disappointed her. "Your mother always gave me an east-facing room."

"Of course." Ashleigh hadn't planned to put Lady Houghton in an east-facing room, but if it made the lady happy, that's exactly what she would do. "Beatrice, please see that Lady Houghton is comfortable in the green room."

"Yes, my lady." Beatrice curtseyed and indicated the stairs while two footmen followed with Lady Houghton's bags.

"Well done," Father whispered to Ashleigh as the elderly woman trailed Beatrice up the grand staircase. He gave her a reassuring smile, but it did little to alleviate her anxiety over the other fifteen houseguests they were expecting.

There would be days of extravagant meals, evening entertainments, sleighrides, ice skating, and droning conversations. To top it all off, a ball was planned for Christmas Eve, the same ball her mother had hosted for twenty-five years, and her mother-in-law before her. The crowning glory of the evening would be the lighting of the Christmas tree, the most dreaded event in Ashleigh's week, because it held such bitter and distasteful memories.

"Ashleigh." Father leaned closer, as if he didn't want the others to hear what he had to say.

"Yes?"

"There's something I've been meaning to tell you for months now." His quiet voice held a hint of trepidation and urgency—a sound she did not like one bit.

"Months?" she whispered. "Why have you waited until this moment to say something?"

Lines of fatigue and grief had aged his distinguished features and his brown hair was almost completely gray now. "I'm afraid I've run out of time."

"Run out of time?" She clutched his arm, fear filling her stomach at the ominous words. "What's wrong, Father?" Was he ill?

A carriage pulled up to the house bearing the Wessex coat of arms. The butler, Mr. Warren, stepped outside into the snow to greet their guests, leaving the large oak door open. Ashleigh caught a glimpse of a tall, handsome man in the carriage.

"Lord Wessex?" she asked quietly, relief making her want to sag. "Is that what you've been wanting to tell me? You invited the most eligible bachelor in London to our house party?" She almost laughed that he'd be so worried about such a thing. Cynthia, Ashleigh's friend and neighbor, would be overjoyed at the news.

Father shook his head. "That's not the surprise that will concern you the most. It's *why* I had to invite him that will upset you."

Two of the Arringtons' footmen met the carriage and opened the door for Eric Easton, the Earl of Wessex, to exit. Ashleigh didn't miss the excited twitter among the maids, nor did she miss the swagger to Eric's shoulders as he nodded a greeting to Mr. Warren and then helped his mother, Lady Wessex, alight from the carriage.

Just seeing the opinionated society matron again caused a shiver to run up Ashleigh's spine. Eric, she could handle, but his mother? The pressure to impress the biggest gossip in England was more than Ashleigh feared she could bear.

"What could be more distressing than Lady Wessex?" Ashleigh asked under her breath. The woman held the power to elevate or destroy Ashleigh's reputation with a flick of her tongue.

Eric and his mother started the trek toward the front door slowly and with great aplomb, four of their personal servants close on their heels.

"The Americans will be joining us for Christmas," Father said just above a whisper.

"The Americans?" Ashleigh frowned, forgetting about Lady Wessex for a moment. "Which Americans?"

"The ones your mother was so fond of."

Ashleigh's eyes widened and all her well-rehearsed manners escaped her as she gasped. "Not the Campbells."

"I'm afraid so." Father sighed.

Christopher Campbell would be in her home for Christmas? The very thought of it made Ashleigh want to disappear to her room for the remainder of the week. The last time she'd seen Christopher was eleven years ago, when she had been eight years old and his family had come to spend the holidays with them. Mrs. Campbell had been one of Mother's oldest and dearest friends, but she had married an American railroad executive and lived in St. Paul, Minnesota. The visit had not gone well—not at all. Christopher had been a horrid boy, just four years older than Ashleigh. He had played tricks on her, caused her to cry, and ultimately ruined Mother's entire Christmas Eve ball by setting the drapes on fire, though no one but Ashleigh knew he was to blame.

Instead, they had all blamed her.

"It's impossible," Ashleigh said with finality. "You must tell them there is no room at Anglesey Abbey."

Father quirked a brow. With over twenty-thousand square meters of living space, it would be impossible to say such a thing.

"I'm afraid it's too late." Father didn't like the Campbells any better than Ashleigh. He had never had anything good to say about the American family her mother loved so well. "They will be here any minute—and I suspect I know why."

"Why?"

Father spoke barely above a whisper as the Eastons drew closer to the house. "Christopher Campbell is coming to fulfill an agreement your mother made with his mother when you two were just children."

"What kind of an agreement?" Ashleigh whispered, not wanting their guests or staff to hear.

Father was very serious as he spoke. "It was your mother's wish, and Mrs. Campbell's wish, that you and Christopher marry—"

"Marry?" Ashleigh forgot herself for a moment and said the word much louder than she intended.

"Shh." Father's expression didn't change as he chastised her. "I suspect they're in need of money and they've come to make good on the agreement. But there is a way out," he said quickly. "The mothers agreed that if either of you were married or engaged to someone else by Christmas Eve 1899, you would not have to go through with their plans. But, if both of you were single..." He let the words trail away.

Ashleigh was single. Very much so. And that was exactly how she wished to stay. She enjoyed the freedom that came with being unencumbered. She had a comfortable home, a doting father, and enough money for the rest of her life. What more did she need?

"Lady Wessex and Lord Wessex." Father looked beyond Ashleigh, a smile plastered to his face. "How nice of you to join us at Anglesey Abbey for Christmas."

Ashleigh had almost forgotten that Lady Wessex was descending upon her house party. She forced herself to smile and turn to their guests, though she could hardly think straight enough to offer the necessary formalities.

Eric Easton was one of the most dashing and elegant men in all of England. He'd been eagerly sought after by dozens of young ladies for the past three years after he'd come into his inheritance and earned the title, Earl of Wessex. But he hadn't settled on a wife—not yet. When he met Ashleigh's gaze, and offered a charming smile, her breath caught. Ever so gallantly, he took her hand to bow over it. "It is a pleasure to be in your company again, Lady Ashleigh. I am looking forward to spending as much time as possible by your side this week."

Father's eyes lit up at the statement and Lady Wessex lifted a disdainful eyebrow.

Ashleigh nodded, hoping her cheeks weren't blooming with color. "Thank you for coming, Lord Wessex." She curtseyed before Eric's mother. "It is a pleasure to have both of you in our home."

Lady Wessex watched Ashleigh closely. "The pleasure is mine, Lady Ashleigh."

"I imagine you'd like to rest before supper," Ashleigh said a bit too quickly. "Mary will take your things to your room."

Ashleigh summoned one of the maids, who blushed and stepped forward to assist Lady Wessex, while the footmen carried their luggage up the wide stairs.

Eric grinned at Ashleigh. "I look forward to seeing you again, soon, Lady Ashleigh."

Her tongue felt tied in knots, so she simply nodded. Oh, how she'd fail miserably at flirting, if it came to that. She'd much rather be in her room drawing, or out of doors, or even in the stable with the horses—anywhere that didn't require her to interact with people and their expectations.

As soon as the Eastons were out of sight,

Father clasped his hands together. "I think there is hope, after all."

"Hope?" Ashleigh wanted to crumple onto the stairway.

"Hope that we can have you engaged by Christmas Eve so you don't have to marry that distasteful Campbell boy and move to America."

Ashleigh's mouth fell open again. Move to America? "What was Mother thinking? Why was I never told?"

Father patted her arm again, as if she were a small child needing comfort. "I suppose she and Mrs. Campbell thought they were doing the best thing for you and Christopher. Though I was against it from the first, I could never say no to her." He sighed. "Now that the time has come, I don't see how we can avoid the agreement—unless you're engaged by Christmas Eve."

It was the last thing she wanted, but it didn't look like she'd have a choice. She just hoped the ill-mannered American didn't ruin her Christmas—again.

∞∞∞

Christopher Campbell had no wish to be in a frigid carriage, traipsing across the snow-covered English countryside. He'd much rather be in London trying to find investors for his railroad. "Will you finally tell me where we're going?" he asked his father, who sat across from him.

"Anglesey Abbey," Father said looking out the window, squinting at the passing village. "You remember the house."

How could he forget? It was the last place he wanted to spend the holidays. "Why couldn't we stay in London? The investment firm could come to a decision any day and I want to be there when they vote."

"So you can be disappointed again?" Father finally met Christopher's gaze. "No one will conduct business this close to Christmas. If they do, you told them where to send for you. But I doubt we'll need to worry about the investment firm. You'll have your money one way or another."

Christopher frowned. "What do you mean by that?"

"Nothing." Father waved his gloved hand in the air, as if to redirect Christopher's attention.

But Christopher sensed it wasn't nothing. "Why are we going to Anglesey Abbey, Father? After what happened the last time we were there, I didn't think you'd ever want to set foot in the Arringtons' home again."

Father was quiet for a moment. "That was eleven years ago. I doubt the Arringtons even remember..." His words died off, but Christopher knew nothing was forgotten.

How could anyone forget that awful Christmas Eve when Christopher had spoiled their party and almost burnt down their home? Mother had been mortified and they had left the following morning, much sooner than planned, to return to St. Paul. But Mother had become sick on the voyage home and died before they'd reached Boston Harbor. Her death wasn't Christopher's fault, he knew that, but she had left her dearest friend in the world on bad terms and they hadn't mended their friendship before she died. The guilt had plagued Christopher his whole life.

"Why would they even invite us?" Christopher asked. The only time they'd heard from the Arringtons since that dreadful night was the announcement of Lady Pemberton's death two years ago.

Father didn't comment, but he tugged on his earlobe, a telltale sign that he was uncomfortable.

Christopher sat up straighter. "They *did* invite us, didn't they?"

"They are expecting us."

Dread mounted in Christopher's chest as he set aside a stack of papers he'd be reading and leaned forward, setting his elbows on his knees. "Did you invite yourself?"

Father settled back on his seat, his countenance aloof. "We have unfinished business, and it couldn't come at a better time."

"What sort of unfinished business?" Christopher had worked with his father in the railroad industry for the past three years since graduating from Harvard. There was little business his father conducted that Christopher didn't know about.

"I suppose you'll learn about it sooner or later." The carriage jostled over the road as they passed the outskirts of the village.

Christopher waited, his patience already thin from their unsuccessful meetings in London. Like so many other American railroad men, they had come to England in search of investments. The Northern Union railroad was the missing link on their tracks from Chicago to Portland, Oregon, but they didn't have the capital to purchase the line. Despite Christopher's early hopes, their meetings had not gone as he had hoped. They had one final investment firm that would take the decision to its board any day. If they said no, Christopher's trip to London would be a complete waste of time and money.

"Last we visited Anglesey Abbey, your mother and Lady Pemberton signed an agreement. We're simply returning to see that the terms of the agreement are fulfilled."

"What kind of an agreement?"

Father reached for his leather bag and pulled out an envelope. He handed it to Christopher. "See for yourself."

Christopher pulled out the single sheet of paper. As he scanned it, his frown deepened, until he shook his head in disbelief and protest. "This can't be true."

"Since you are not married or engaged, we are going to Anglesey Abbey to see if Lady Ashleigh is single as well. If she is, then you will work out the terms of your engagement and announce it on Christmas Eve." Father smiled, though it wasn't a look of joy that one would expect when speaking of his son's engagement—but one of triumph, as if besting a foe. "Once an engagement is announced in England, there is no backing out. Unless the person who forfeits the engagement wants their reputation to be forever tarnished and a breach of contract case on their hands."

"This isn't a legally binding contract," Christopher said, his pulse starting to slow. "Even if it was, there would be some way to get out of the agreement."

Father leaned forward. "You're right. It's not legally binding. But it was your mother's last wish that you and Lady Ashleigh marry." He stared at Christopher with the same look of disappointment he'd given him as they'd driven away from Anglesey Abbey the last time. "You wouldn't want to dishonor your mother's memory by saying no."

Guilt washed over Christopher. The least he could do was honor his mother's last wish—yet, he had no desire to marry. He spent almost all of his waking hours at his office. He had no time or space in his life for a wife, let alone Ashleigh Arrington! The girl had been a tattletale, getting him in trouble for things he hadn't even done wrong. He couldn't stand the sight of her when they'd visited Anglesey Abbey eleven years ago. How much worse she must be as a persnickety woman.

"I couldn't possibly get married. Especially to Ashleigh."

"Think long and hard about that decision." Father's voice was low and serious. "Ashleigh Arrington is the only child of Lord Pemberton, one of the wealthiest men in England. An alliance with him would ensure all the investment we would ever need for our railroads."

Christopher shook his head. "I wouldn't even think of marrying for financial gain." His parents had married for that very reason, and Christopher didn't have a single happy memory of his parents from childhood because of it. Theirs had been a strained relationship, with no love, and little tolerance for one another. Nothing in life was worth that kind of trouble.

"It doesn't matter what you think," Father said, settling back into his bench seat. "The agreement was made by your mother and Lady Pemberton. Whether you want this to happen or not, it may be out of your hands. Lord Pemberton is honor bound to see it through."

Anglesey Abbey appeared in the distance, its towers, gothic architecture, and brownstone exterior jutting out from the rolling countryside.

Lady Ashleigh was probably awaiting his arrival eagerly. No doubt she was in need of a husband. What man in his right mind would marry that woman? A successful, unsuspecting American was probably just the person her father was hoping to come along and take her off his hands.

The carriage slowed and turned onto the gravel driveway leading to Anglesey Abbey. They drove through the gatehouse, which was open and welcoming, the gatekeeper waving at the driver as they passed.

"I can't get married," Christopher said again, a hint of desperation in his voice. "We'll simply have to explain that the agreement is...is..."

"What?" Father shook his head. "A foolish decision made by two loving, devoted mothers?" He frowned. "You'd bring shame upon your mother, Lady Pemberton, and Lady Ashleigh if you tried to back out now."

The carriage rolled closer to Anglesey Abbey. The front door opened and a man stepped outside, his black suit in contrast to the snow-white landscape. He stood at attention, waiting for the carriage to come to a stop.

"I didn't think this trip to England could get any worse," Christopher said under his breath. Not only did he still need to secure investment for his railroad, but he'd have to find some way to get out of this ridiculous agreement.

"Remember this is the first Christmas they're celebrating since Lady Pemberton's death," Father said. "We don't want to add to their grief, if we don't have to."

Christopher wanted to groan when the carriage finally stopped and the door was opened by the servant.

"Welcome to Anglesey Abbey," the servant

said. "I'm Mr. Warren, the butler. If there is anything you need, please don't hesitate to ask."

Christopher steeled himself from the coming encounter with Lady Ashleigh, and remembered his manners. "Thank you."

He stepped out of the carriage, trying not to look too melancholy or frustrated. If the Arringtons hadn't invited them, how would they be received? What an awkward position Father had put them in.

Father exited the carriage. "Come, Christopher."

Gravel crunched under their feet as they walked toward the front door. An older gentleman and young lady stood just inside the foyer, though he couldn't make out any details. All he recalled about Ashleigh was her wiry blond hair, her flashing brown eyes, and the spray of freckles across her stub of a nose. She had been whiny, obnoxious, and annoying.

Dread mixed with impatience and frustration. This was the last thing Christopher needed to deal with this week. Even though he had instructed the investment firm to contact him when they planned to vote, he was still four hours away from London. Close, but not close enough.

"Here we go," Father said.

"Mr. Campbell, how nice of you to come." Lord Pemberton's voice was aristocratic and tight as he greeted Father. "I believe you remember my daughter, Lady Ashleigh."

"Lord Pemberton, Lady Ashleigh." When

Father bowed, Christopher had his first full look at Ashleigh in eleven years—and he almost tripped over his own feet.

Gone was the gangly, awkward child. In her place stood a beautiful young woman.

"And you remember my son, Christopher?" Father asked.

"It's good to see you again, Christopher." Lord Arrington nodded, though he didn't smile. "Ashleigh and I are very glad you've come."

Christopher met Ashleigh's brown-eyed gaze. He could hardly believe the woman before him was the same child who had caused so much grief last time he had visited. "Lady Ashleigh, it's a pleasure to see you again."

She stood tall and slender, her soft blond curls secure in a becoming hairstyle, her freckles a distant memory on her clear skin. The stub little nose was now an elegant complement to her lovely face.

"Mr. Campbell." She offered her hand and he bowed over it. "The pleasure is all mine."

She spoke the words so elegantly and deliberately, Christopher sensed they were not genuine. Was she happy to see him? Surely, she recalled their last meeting with the same distaste as he. Thankfully he wasn't the spoiled boy he'd been—but she wouldn't know that.

After the initial greeting, an uncomfortable silence filled the air as the four looked at one another. Christopher couldn't help but glance at her ring finger—and saw it was empty.

She slipped her hand into the folds of her fetching gown.

It didn't mean she wasn't engaged, or at least spoken for. But how would he find out?

"It's been so long since your last visit," Lord Pemberton said. "Much has changed these eleven years."

More than Christopher ever imagined.

"I'm sorry for your loss." Father sounded genuine. "Lady Pemberton will be missed."

"Thank you." Lord Pemberton's face was stoic as he spoke. He didn't offer any more or any less.

Again, silence descended.

"We hope you'll have a pleasant stay," Ashleigh finally said. "One of the footmen will show you to your rooms."

Christopher longed to speak to her about the agreement, yet he didn't think it was right to bring it up in front of the servants or so soon after their arrival. "I look forward to speaking to you later this evening, if I may."

She studied him with her dark eyes, distrust and apprehension wavering in their depths. "I will be very busy this evening, but perhaps we can arrange a few moments."

If that was all she'd give him, then it would be enough. It had to be enough. The sooner he could get out of the agreement, the better.

Chapter Two

"Shall we?" Father offered his arm to Ashleigh just outside the drawing room where all of their guests had gathered before dinner.

With a steadying breath and a quick nod, she took his offered arm and drew strength knowing she wasn't alone.

Father took a step and then paused. "Remember what you need to do tonight. The Campbells have come to arrange a marriage between you and Christopher, but we still have three days before they can make any demands."

What could they possibly demand? Ashleigh had read the copy of the document her mother and Mrs. Campbell had signed. It wasn't legal, simply a formality. The Campbells couldn't force her hand. But Ashleigh couldn't deny it was her mother's wish, either. The last thing she wanted was to disappoint her mother, even if her mother was no longer with them.

"Eric Easton comes from a good family, with a

good title." Father squeezed her arm for reassurance. "He would be my choice."

Ashleigh hardly knew the man, but she would do her best to rectify that problem. "Let's go in."

Mr. Warren stood just outside the drawing room with the first footman nearby. They opened the gilded doors to allow Ashleigh and her father to enter.

The north drawing room was one of Ashleigh's favorites at Anglesey Abbey, especially now, trimmed for the holidays. Large and airy, with cream-colored walls and gold trim, it bespoke of the rich heritage of the Arrington family and the women who had put their special touch in selecting the elegant furniture that graced the room. Ashleigh had overseen the decorations and ordered an abundance of fresh pine boughs, which fragranced the air.

Here and there, the guests had assembled in small groups. Women wore glittering jewelry, golden tiaras, and long white gloves. The men were resplendent in black evening coats and shiny black shoes. Laughter and conversation filled the room, but several people noticed their arrival and stopped to nod a greeting.

Ashleigh intended to meet Eric's gaze, but it was Christopher that caught her attention. He stood a head taller than all the other guests, his dark brown hair combed back into perfect submission, his intense blue eyes studying the room, the people, and then finally her. There was a directness about him that was both irritating and intriguing. She was reminded again how much he had changed. He'd always been a handsome, though insufferable, boy. But now, he was dashing, strong, and confident. It would be impossible to miss him in a crowd.

"Lady Ashleigh." Eric approached and bowed before her.

Father stepped away and joined another conversation, leaving Ashleigh alone with Eric.

It was time to turn on the charm she didn't possess and try to attract the attention of a man she didn't want to marry. The very thought of it made her tremble. How did a person go about flirting? She'd watched countless women at countless balls and social gatherings, but she'd found their conduct to be ridiculous and embarrassing most of the time. She couldn't bring herself to match their behavior —no matter how much she wanted to honor her mother.

"Lord Wessex." She curtseyed. At least she knew how to do that properly.

"Lady Ashleigh, you look lovely this evening."

"Thank you." Ashleigh's maid had taken great pains with her appearance this evening. Her green gown had been made just for the occasion.

Cynthia hovered nearby, as if waiting for an invitation to join the conversation. Relief flooded Ashleigh. Her friend could help her. "Cynthia!"

Cynthia glided over, her cheeks pink and her green eyes glowing. She offered Eric an elegant curtsey. "Good evening, Lord Wessex. It's wonderful to see you again."

"Lady Cynthia." Eric bowed, his lips tight. "It's a pleasure to see you again, as well."

Ashleigh should have been focused on Eric, but Christopher had not stopped watching her since she'd entered the drawing room.

She knew, because she couldn't keep her eyes off of him, no matter how hard she tried.

He started toward her group, his intent clear. He was coming to speak with her. Panic seized Ashleigh. Would he want to discuss the marriage agreement here, now? It wouldn't be the time or the place for such things, but Americans were so vulgar and direct in their dealings. She couldn't be too sure.

"Would you excuse me?" Ashleigh said quickly. "I need to see to one of my guests." If Christopher was determined to speak with her, she wanted as few ears to hear as possible.

Eric frowned and his gaze traveled across the room to where Christopher was advancing. "Of course, though I do hope we'll get a chance to speak later."

Ashleigh nodded and moved away to meet Christopher in the center of the room. Her heart beat an unsteady rhythm at the determination in his eyes. What would she do if anyone discovered the real reason this man and his father were visiting? She must keep it a secret and hope he didn't make his intentions known. Once the rumors started, it would be impossible to attract another man's attention.

"Mr. Campbell," she said almost breathlessly. "I hope your room is to your liking."

"Anglesey Abbey is just as beautiful as the last time I was here. It hasn't changed a bit."

Memories of his last visit surfaced and her anxiety was soon replaced with irritation. She lifted her chin. "The ballroom parlor is quite altered. If you recall, we had a fire there the last time you visited. It required extensive renovations."

"How could I forget?" A shadow passed over his face as he frowned. "I never did get a chance to apologize for all of that. I'm sorry."

Ashleigh's mouth parted in surprise. It was the last thing she expected him to say. "Yes, well, nothing was broken that couldn't be mended." Except her mother's shame in Ashleigh. It was the last time she ever asked Ashleigh to put the star on the top of the tree, or perform any other social obligation that would require Ashleigh to be the center of attention. Mother didn't want Ashleigh to embarrass her again.

All formality slipped away and Christopher leaned closer to Ashleigh. "Is there somewhere we could speak privately? There is much to discuss, and I would like to get it over with as soon as possible."

Ashleigh's jaw tightened as several people stopped to listen to their conversation. "I'm afraid that isn't possible right now," she said through clenched teeth. "Dinner is about to be served."

"Then when? I would like to return to London, but it's my understanding that there is an agreement

—"

"Please." Ashleigh shook her head and frowned, her body temperature rising. "Now is not the time."

Christopher straightened and nodded, frustration in the lines of his face. "Fine. But it must be tonight. I'd like to take care of this situation sooner than later."

Sooner than later? Didn't she have until Christmas Eve?

Mr. Warren stepped into the room at that moment and clasped his hands. "Dinner is served."

Ashleigh was never so happy to hear those words in her life.

Father stepped forward and offered his arm to escort Lady Wessex into the dining room and Ashleigh joined Lord Majorly, the Count of Harmony Hall, who would escort her.

Eric offered his arm to Cynthia, who smiled up at the handsome young man in complete adoration.

Ashleigh was no closer to securing Eric's proposal than she had been when she entered the room.

It would be a long night, especially if she had the conversation with Christopher to dread.

The candles danced and flickered, reflecting off the large windows in the north drawing room.

Christopher sat in one corner, on a surprisingly comfortable chair—the first one he'd found at Anglesey Abbey—and watched the young adults play Blindman's Bluff after supper. Besides himself and Ashleigh, there were six others in the room. Christopher had chosen not to participate, hoping to get time alone with Ashleigh, instead. She, on the other hand, seemed content to avoid him. She stood in the opposite corner of the room, overseeing the game, though she didn't participate.

Laughter and conversation filled the room. Christopher was the only stranger among the group, and the houseguests had tried to draw him out, but he had a different type of game to play tonight. One that was much more important and carried far heavier consequences.

His state of matrimony—or lack thereof.

Ashleigh glanced in his direction again, but this time Christopher had had enough. He left the comfort of his chair and walked along the outside of the room, narrowly missing the young lady who was blindfolded, her fingers outstretched and wiggling for effect.

As he drew closer, Ashleigh's eyes grew wider. She started to move away from her place near the door, but he stepped in her way.

"How long must we play cat and mouse, Lady Ashleigh?" he asked quietly, for her ears alone.

Her large brown eyes blinked up at him in confusion. "Whatever do you mean, Mr. Campbell?"

"Each time I make an advance to speak to

you, you either skitter away, or distract me from my objective." He studied her, surprised again by how much she had changed over the years. "I would like a private audience with you."

Her gaze circled the room. "It wouldn't be seemly to leave my guests, or be alone with you."

"Then let's just step outside the drawing room and leave the door open." He wanted to return to London in the morning. They must talk now.

She clasped her hands and looked around the room again. She didn't act the way he'd imagined when his father told him about the agreement. Christopher had expected an overzealous woman, hanging on his arm, following his every footstep.

Ashleigh Arrington was anything but eager to be by his side—or any other man's in this room. Instead, she seemed content to avoid them all together.

"I suppose we can't put it off forever." She nodded toward the door and led the way. "We will speak in the hall." She paused. "With the door open."

"Of course."

He followed her into the dimly lit hall. It ran the length of the main floor of Anglesey Abbey, with the large staircase at one end and the front doors at the other. The marble floors were polished and the high ceilings echoed with their footsteps. It wasn't the ideal place to have an intimate conversation, but it would have to do.

Christopher squared his shoulders. He would have to tackle this problem just like he did all the other obstacles he came across in his business dealings. Straightforward, level-headed, and without emotions getting in his way.

Ashleigh turned and clasped her hands again, but she didn't speak. She only looked at him with those clear, steady eyes.

Christopher opened his mouth to address the situation at hand, but didn't know quite where to begin. Her calm confidence unraveled him. "I assume you are aware of the agreement our mothers made when we were children?"

"Yes."

"How long have you known?"

"I learned of it moments before you arrived this afternoon."

Was that defiance in her voice?

Christopher frowned. If she'd only just learned of the agreement, then perhaps she hadn't been eagerly anticipating his arrival. Maybe she was just as bewildered as him. "And you're not happy about the arrangement?"

She slowly tilted her chin up, though there was something vulnerable in her eyes. "I have no wish to marry anyone at this time."

He stared at her for a moment, relief flooding through him. "Neither do I."

Her brown eyes lit up with hope and her chin lowered. "Truly?"

"I only just learned about it moments before we arrived." He almost laughed at the absurdity of the whole ordeal. He'd allowed himself to get riled up for nothing. "My father..." His words trailed away as he recalled the conversation he'd had with his father earlier.

"Your father?" she asked, her gaze searching his face.

Christopher shook his head. His father had reminded him that he owed it to his mother's memory to honor her last request. How could he not?

The sinking feeling returned. Even if Ashleigh wasn't agreeable to the arrangement, what did it matter? It was his mother's last request.

"My father told me that our mothers signed the agreement just a few days before we left Anglesey Abbey the last time." He hated the feeling of guilt that slayed him every time he thought about that last week before his mother died. He'd been such a disappointment to her.

Ashleigh nodded. "I believe my father mentioned that as well."

Christopher walked away, his footsteps echoing in the massive space. He ran his hand through his hair and rested it at the base of his neck. "She wanted this match more than anything."

There was a pause before Ashleigh spoke again. "What are you suggesting?"

He turned and couldn't miss her cautious gaze. "I don't believe I could ignore this agreement in good conscience. Not when it came from my mother."

She lowered her lashes and let out a sigh. "I

suppose I could not, either."

Her simple statement tugged at his heart.

There was something about this young woman that drew Christopher. As he'd watched her during supper, and then in the drawing room, she hadn't tried to stand out or be noticed, but neither had she shied away from attention. She was graceful and confident, yet she had a humility about her that was very attractive.

"Where does that leave us?" he asked.

Ashleigh clasped and unclasped her hands and then looked toward the drawing room.

Lord Wessex was blindfolded, chasing the young ladies.

"There is still time, before the deadline," she said. "My father has made his wishes known, so I will pursue the man he has chosen." She squared her shoulders. "If all goes as planned, I'll be engaged to someone else by Christmas Eve and you and I will be free of the agreement."

Lord Wessex peeked out from beneath the blindfold as he cornered one lady after another. "Where has Lady Ashleigh run off to?" he asked.

Lady Cynthia pointed toward the hall and Lord Wessex turned on his heel and started in their direction. "She cannot hide for long," he said.

Even in the faded light of the hall, Christopher saw the telltale shade of pink on Ashleigh's cheeks.

"Wessex?" he asked. "Has he proposed?"

"A lady doesn't speak of such things," Ashleigh said quietly.

"You and I can forgo such formalities, Ashleigh." He spoke her name freely. "We are in this thing together, for better or worse, until one of us gets engaged. We might as well work together."

Lord Wessex came to the door and lifted his head to peek out from beneath the blindfold again. When he saw Christopher, he took off the scarf and frowned. "Is everything all right, Lady Ashleigh?"

"Everything is fine, thank you." Her smile looked forced and uncomfortable. "We'll return to the drawing room presently."

Lord Wessex studied Christopher, the slightest scowl on his face, but he bowed to Ashleigh and returned to the drawing room without another word.

Ashleigh took a step toward Christopher, her face serious, her voice low. "I don't like this agreement any more than you, Christopher." She said his first name a bit awkwardly. "But it is none of your concern whom I plan to pursue." She swallowed and glanced at the door where Lord Wessex had stood a moment before. If she was this nervous and uncomfortable simply talking about pursuing the man, how would she accomplish her goal?

She offered a curtsey. "Now, if you'll excuse me." She walked away, her back straight and her shoulders stiff.

For all her elegance and grace, she didn't appear to know the fine art of flirtation. Lord Wessex, on the other hand, had practice beyond his years.

Christopher sighed. Just like all his other business dealings, he'd have to keep a close eye on this situation. If he didn't stay at Anglesey Abbey to ensure Ashleigh's success at securing a proposal from Lord Wessex, Christopher might be the one with a wife at the end of the week.

An unwelcome prospect, to say the least.

Chapter Three

From a distance, Anglesey Abbey looked like a fairytale castle up on the hill, the setting sun casting shades of purple, pink, and orange across the vast winter sky. Ashleigh stretched out her hands toward the crackling bonfire near the edge of the frozen pond, warming her fingers and taking a moment to simply enjoy the scene before her.

It was the second day of the house party, and the younger guests had traversed the snow-packed road from the house down to the pond, ice skates slung over their shoulders. A roaring fire had already been laid by the servants, and the party had enjoyed hot cocoa before donning their skates to take to the ice. Eric and Cynthia glided along, their eyes glowing and their cheeks tinged with pink. Ashleigh had yet to put on her skates, preferring the quiet of the fire after the busy morning and afternoon of playing cards, visiting with the older guests, and overseeing breakfast and lunch.

Christopher sat on a bench near the edge of

the pond and attached his blades onto the bottom of his shoes. He'd spent the day with everyone else, but hadn't tried speaking to her again. His father, on the other hand, had been by her side most of the morning, telling her all about life in America.

"Would you like to skate?" Christopher asked when he caught her watching him. He straightened and lifted her skates, which were lying on the bench near him. "I'd be happy to help you with your blades."

Cynthia laughed as she clung to Eric's arm, flailing about as if she didn't know how to skate, when Ashleigh knew full well that she was an excellent skater. Eric grinned down at Cynthia and then wrapped his arm around her waist to help her along.

If Ashleigh didn't do something soon, she'd lose her chance with Eric—and then who would be left? One of the other bachelors who was visiting? She quickly perused the options and shuddered. None of the other men appealed to her.

She was coming to accept that she might have to act like Cynthia, after all. Feign weakness, ignorance, and inability. If it meant attracting Eric's attention, then she'd have no choice.

"I'd love to skate." Ashleigh left the fire and took a seat next to Christopher. "But I don't need any help putting them on, thank you."

He tightened the straps over his boots and nodded. "It's refreshing to know a woman who can take care of herself."

Ashleigh attached the blades to the bottom of her boots, tightening the straps for support. "Do you keep company with weak women?"

He laughed. "Ah, no. I don't have much acquaintance with women in general, but when I do, I find them to be tedious and needy."

She sat up straighter, irritation prickling her spine. "Not all women, surely."

Cynthia continued to giggle beside Eric, leaning into him for support, smiling up in adoration, her skates slipping out from beneath her from time to time.

Christopher looked away from Cynthia and stood, his left eyebrow quirked. "Not all women— but most." He extended his hand. "Shall we?"

Ashleigh lifted her chin and stood without his assistance. "I'm quite capable of standing on my own."

His eyes twinkled and his lips twitched. "Would you like me to escort you onto the ice? Or are you capable of that, as well?"

She pinched her lips together and scowled, but it only increased his merriment.

He stepped aside and offered a slight bow. "Don't let me get in your way."

She started toward the frozen pond, her head high and her back straight. It took a bit of concentration to stay balanced on the blades, but she'd had enough practice over the years to manage without assistance.

Christopher walked close behind, but she

didn't bother to speak to him as they followed the path the others had already broken in the snow.

Her clothing was stylish and warm, lined in brown fur and velvet, but it didn't stop the wind from nipping at her nose or ruffling her skirts. The crackle of the fire begged her to return, but she had a job to do, and she aimed to do it. Today. This very moment. She'd flirt with Eric, even if it was the last thing she did.

As she came to the banks of the pond, she estimated the drop from land to ice to be at least a foot. All the other women had accepted a helping hand down, but one look at the bemused expression on Christopher's face made her decide to do it herself.

She anchored her right foot into the packed snow, bent her knee, and put her left foot onto the ice.

"Oh, Ashleigh!" Cynthia waved from across the pond. "You're joining us!"

Eric glanced toward Ashleigh, so she waved her gloved hand and tried to look coquettish—however that looked—and immediately lost her precarious balance on the ice.

Her left foot slipped out from beneath her, but her right foot was still anchored to the land.

A startled cry left her lips as she flailed her arms to regain her balance—but it was no use. She came down hard on her backside, while her right ankle twisted in protest.

Before Ashleigh could gather her senses,

Christopher was by her side in the snow, concern wedged between his eyes. "My goodness, Ashleigh. Are you hurt?"

Pain radiated up her right leg, but she couldn't admit that she was hurt—especially when she'd been so stubborn and gotten herself into this mess.

"Ashleigh, darling!" Cynthia broke away from Eric's side and sped across the ice, coming to a magnificent halt within half a meter of Ashleigh. She knelt before her in a puddle of purple skirts, her green eyes filled with worry. "Did you hurt yourself?"

"Help me up, will you?" Ashleigh asked her friend.

Cynthia rose to lend a hand, but Christopher was already by her side. He reached beneath her arms and lifted her to her feet.

Embarrassment warmed Ashleigh's cheeks as she readjusted her skirts and managed to say, "Thank you."

Eric and the others joined them on the edge of the pond, concern in their gazes.

She had to put most of her weight on her left foot, which was difficult in the skate. "I'm quite all right." She forced a smile. "Truly. Everyone, go back to your fun."

"Are you certain?" Cynthia asked.

"I'm fine." Her pride refused to share the truth. "Just a little bruised. I'll return to the house and wait for you to join me later."

"You can't return alone." Eric stepped

forward. "I'd be happy to escort you."

"That won't be necessary." Ashleigh didn't want the others to see her shame—especially Eric. If he walked her back, he'd know she was more injured than she let on. She tried to put weight on her injured ankle, but winced at the pain. She couldn't very well walk back on her own. "Mr. Campbell will accompany me to the house."

Christopher raised his eyebrows. "Wouldn't you rather go with Lord Wessex?"

"Who will help Lady Cynthia skate if Lord Wessex returns with me?" Ashleigh asked with forced laughter in her voice, desperate not to embarrass herself in front of Eric any further.

Christopher frowned, but bent over to unstrap his skates. "As you wish."

Eric shook his head. "I insist."

Cynthia wrapped her hands around Eric's arm once again and smiled up at him. "We'll join Ashleigh and Mr. Campbell a bit later, just as Ashleigh suggested." She skated backward, pulling Eric along with her, and for once, Ashleigh was thankful her friend was dominating Eric's time and attention.

The others moved away as well, leaving Ashleigh alone with Christopher once again.

"I thought you wanted Lord Wessex's attention," he said quietly. "Why didn't you take his offer?"

She tried to put weight on her ankle to get to the bench. "I'd prefer he didn't see me embarrass myself."

Christopher's eyes wrinkled at the corners as he smiled. "But you don't mind if I do?"

"You've seen me at my worst already." Reminders of the last time he visited returned. She'd never been more embarrassed in her life than the night he set their Christmas tree and drapes on fire.

"Here." He bent down and put her right arm over his shoulder. "I'll help you back to the bench to take off your skates."

He was much taller than she was, so it was a bit awkward, but he helped her hobble to the bench. She tried hard not to limp, in case the others watched, but it was almost impossible.

She sat on the bench and he knelt before her to loosen the straps.

After a moment, he chuckled. "I find it exceedingly ironic that you refused my help fastening your skates, but now you're forced to accept my help in taking them off."

Irritation stiffened her back and she leaned over. "I am quite capable of taking off my own skates, Mr. Campbell."

He gently pushed her hands aside. "Don't be stubborn, Ashleigh." He looked up and met her gaze, his blue eyes quite serious—and altogether too handsome. "I want to help you."

Her cheeks warmed and she looked away.

When he was done, he offered his hand. "You've changed in so many other ways, it's a bit refreshing to know you're still as stubborn as before."

She stood. "I prefer to think of myself as determined."

"Call it what you will," he said, a smile in his voice. "Are you able to walk on your own?"

Ashleigh put a bit of weight on the tender ankle and winced, but she nodded. "I believe I can."

"No, you can't." Without asking, Christopher swept her off her feet and held her in his arms.

She was breathless as her face came inches away from his.

"You wear your emotions on your face, did you know that?" he asked quietly.

She blinked several times before she had the wherewithal to protest, though it was weak, at best. "Put me down, Mr. Campbell. I said I could walk."

"What you say"—he began to walk toward Anglesey Abbey—"and what your face tells me, are two different things." He met her gaze, his mouth quirked. "Your pride knows no bounds, Lady Ashleigh, but there's no need to pretend." He bent his head a little closer to hers in a conspiratorial way. "You don't need to impress me."

She crossed her arms and directed her gaze away from him, setting her mouth in a firm line. "I'm not trying to impress anyone."

"Really?" He continued to walk, following the path they'd taken to reach the pond. It was a dreadfully long road, uphill, but it didn't seem to affect him at all. "Isn't this whole party meant to impress these people?"

"I'm simply trying to create a pleasant experience for my friends."

"Is that what this is all about?" He shook his head. "You could have fooled me. I assumed you were trying to recreate the famous house parties your mother gave. With her gone, I imagine there is a very heavy weight upon your shoulders to impress the ton. You're trying very hard, aren't you?"

Ashleigh's arms went limp. "Is it that obvious?"

His features softened and he shook his head. "No. I just assumed."

She sighed and nibbled her bottom lip. If her ankle was hurt badly, it would be impossible to play hostess for the rest of the week. Everyone would have to go home.

How would she find a way to flirt with Eric then?

"You're doing a fine job, Ashleigh." He tightened his hold on her and smiled. "You've been impressing me from the moment I arrived."

Ashleigh warmed at his compliment.

"Especially when you fell so gracefully just now." He grinned. "It was quite impressive, if I must say so."

She narrowed her eyes again and lightly punched his shoulder, but couldn't stop from joining in his laughter.

It felt good to know that Christopher wasn't the bully he used to be.

But she wasn't quite sure what he was

anymore.

∞ ∞ ∞

The doctor had come and gone, but Ashleigh didn't like what he had to say, so she chose to ignore him.

"Why I even called for the doctor is a mystery," Father had said earlier when she'd met him in the hallway to go down to dinner. "Didn't he advise you to stay off your ankle for the remainder of the week?"

"Fiddlesticks." Her maid, Mary, had bound the ankle in a tight bandage, and Ashleigh had tried to overlook the discomfort as she walked beside her father. "It's simply a sprain. I've been icing it all afternoon. I'll be fine."

He had shaken his head, but didn't speak of it further.

Now, with supper behind them, they had all gone to the north parlor where they would pass the evening with songs, recitations, and games.

The room was warm, heated by the oversized fireplace and the dozens of candles in the wall sconces. Pine garland was draped across the fireplace mantel and mistletoe hung over the entrance to the door. A footman stood at attention near the table where hot apple cider was being served, while Ashleigh's guests sat in small groups around the room.

Ashleigh finally had Eric's attention as they

sat on a sofa, discussing the plans that Ashleigh had made for the next day. He had come to inquire about her ankle, but she had artfully directed the conversation away from her embarrassing escapades.

"I've heard you're an accomplished violinist, Mr. Campbell," Cynthia said over the din of conversation, clapping her hands in excitement. "Will you play for us?"

Christopher sat at a table in the corner of the room with his father and another older gentleman, a deck of cards in hand. Ashley noticed he had been watching her and Eric. She had caught his broody glances as the evening progressed. He looked up now at Cynthia's request. "Accomplished is too kind a word. Dabble is more appropriate."

A vague memory started to form in Ashleigh's mind. The last time he'd visited, she recalled walking into the music room on the third floor of Anglesey Abbey, drawn there by the most hauntingly beautiful sound she'd ever heard. Christopher had been standing near a window, an ebony violin in hand. He had been playing a song she'd never heard before. His face had been serene, almost peaceful, and she'd been surprised to find the annoying boy had a tender side, after all. She hadn't moved a muscle, afraid he'd know she was standing there. Even then, as a boy of twelve, he'd played the violin better than anyone she'd ever heard.

"Do play for us, Mr. Campbell," Ashleigh said with a sudden longing to hear him again.

He studied her for a moment, a twinkle forming in his eyes. "Only if you'll sing for us."

Heat filled her cheeks as another memory surfaced. He'd come across her singing to one of her kittens in the barn on that long-ago visit and had teased her incessantly.

Did he intend to tease her again?

"If I recall," he said, rising to his feet, "you have a lovely voice."

"Oh, please do," Cynthia begged Ashleigh.

Others joined in, but it was Eric's encouragement that finally persuaded Ashleigh to agree. If she could please Eric, then it would be worth all the teasing she'd have to endure from Christopher.

She stood. "All right."

The group cheered and Eric smiled.

"I'll go and retrieve my violin." Christopher stopped by her side on his way out of the parlor and spoke quietly for her ears alone. "I've been waiting eleven years to hear you sing again."

She couldn't tell if he teased, or if he was sincere. Before she could discern his meaning, he left the room.

Eric stood while the others spoke in excited tones around the candlelit room. The shadows played about the planes of his face, accentuating his fine features. He was almost too pretty, truth be told, but it added to his magnetic charm. She was quite certain that every young lady in the room was smitten with the handsome earl. And she was running out of time. She must try flirting with him again.

"I've heard that you have a fine voice, as well, Lord Wessex." She blinked her eyes, hoping her eyelashes would flutter. "Will you sing for us this evening?"

"I might." He frowned and leaned forward. "Is there something in your eye, Lady Ashleigh?"

She stopped fluttering her eyes and opened them wide, shaking her head. "No." Embarrassment flooded her face with heat. "I simply..." What? Simply what?

"Yes?" he asked.

"I simply—nothing." She laughed, wanting to sound as lyrical as Cynthia, but it came out a bit awkward. "Did you enjoy ice skating today?"

"Yes." His face smoothed and he leaned closer, his voice deepening. "I've enjoyed everything about my activities at Anglesey Abbey—except for the times you haven't been with me."

She knew he was flirting—it was painfully obvious—but she didn't know how to respond. Oh! If only this came naturally to her. "Well, that's— wonderful," she said a bit too loud. "I'm happy to hear it."

"Ashleigh." He paused. "I may call you Ashleigh?"

She swallowed. "Yes—yes, of course." Why did her pulse beat so strongly in her ears, and why did her voice quiver? No doubt her cheeks were pink.

"Then you must call me Eric."

She began to grow overly warm near the fireplace. Where was Christopher with that violin? "A-All right," she stammered, rubbing her sweating palms down her skirt.

"Ashleigh," he said again, taking a step closer to her, clearly wanting the others to be excluded from this conversation. "I've been meaning to speak to you privately since arriving."

He had?

"But every time I turn around, Mr. Campbell seems to have your undivided attention."

"Yes, well." She took a step back, but immediately wished she hadn't. She was supposed to give Eric the impression that she wanted his advances, didn't she? Without thinking, she stepped forward, her ankle protesting, to be even closer to Eric than she'd been before.

His frown returned and she wanted to crawl under the rug.

Now she stood too close to him. He must think her a complete ninny.

"I have been trying to devote my time to *all* my guests," she said.

"Yet, I haven't had nearly enough of your attention."

His words made the heat gather under her collar. "Lord Wessex."

"Eric," he said quietly, dramatically.

Cynthia watched them closely from the opposite side of the room, though the others pretended not to notice. Could they hear him?

What must they all think with Ashleigh standing so close to him?

"Your words lead me to believe..." Ashleigh let her comment trail away, because she didn't know how to finish the sentence. Was he interested in her? Was there hope that he might propose? How did she ask such a delicate question?

If only she could know for certain. She would be free of the marriage agreement with Christopher.

"Lead you to believe what?" Eric asked. "That I —"

"Why wait for my son to return?" Mr. Campbell stood to his feet and spoke in a loud voice. "Lady Ashleigh, will you sing for us now?"

Ashleigh wanted to cry out in relief, and sigh in frustration. What had Eric been about to say? She half hoped and half dreaded what it might be.

Eric was forced to move aside so Ashleigh could answer the older gentleman. It would be rude to deny his request, but she wanted to know what Eric was about to say.

"Wouldn't you rather I wait for Mr. Campbell to return with his violin?" she asked. "I'd sound much better accompanied by music."

"I'll accompany you on the pianoforte." Cynthia quickly took a seat at the large instrument. "What shall I play, Ashleigh? 'God Rest Ye, Merry Gentlemen'? 'Hark! The Harold, Angels Sing'?"

The others waited in expectation.

"Excuse me, Lord Wessex." Ashleigh took a step around him, trying not to limp. "Whatever you prefer, Cynthia."

Cynthia offered a satisfied smile and began to play 'Good King Wenceslas.'

After a few popular carols, Christopher returned and Cynthia quietly left the pianoforte to take a spot near Eric on a sofa facing the fireplace.

Large snowflakes began to fall outside, brushing the oversized windows on their way to the ground. Inside, the fireplace crackled while Christopher took his violin out of its case.

The look of reverence on his face made Ashleigh recall the way he'd held and played the violin as a child. When he lifted it to his chin and laid the bow across the strings, he closed his eyes briefly and let out a sigh, though she didn't think he even realized it.

After a few notes and a little tuning, he lowered the instrument and smiled at Ashleigh. "What would you like to sing?"

She'd rather listen to him play, but he had asked her to sing, so she would. "'Silent Night'?"

He nodded. "My favorite."

It was her favorite as well.

The violin came up again. He waited just a moment until she rose and joined him, indicating that she was ready, then he began to play.

The sound was exquisite, just as she remembered. Beneath his expert hands, the notes became at once joyful and melancholy, as if he poured his very soul into the music. She found her voice following the ebb and flow of the emotions, caught up in the moment.

Silent night, holy night,
All is calm, all is bright...

The others faded and it became just the two of them. She couldn't take her eyes off him as he played the familiar song in a way that was his very own. His pensive gaze never strayed from her face.

When it came to an end, they stared at one another. The others remained quiet for a heartbeat, but then they began to applaud and call for an encore.

For once, Christopher didn't smile or tease as he watched her.

Something had happened while they sang. Something she could not define—or maybe she didn't want to.

Whatever it was, it both scared her and made her feel as if she could fly.

Chapter Four

Long after everyone had gone to bed, Christopher stood in the north parlor watching the snowflakes dance against the windowpanes.

His violin had been returned to its case, the fireplace had been banked by a servant, and the candles had been extinguished. Still, he stood near the window, his mind too awake to find rest.

"I thought I might find you here." Ashleigh's voice was quiet, almost reverent in the stillness of the late hour.

Christopher took a long breath before he turned to look at her.

She had taken his breath away more than once that evening. First, when she'd appeared in a stunning gown in the drawing room before dinner, second, when she'd mesmerized the entire room by singing "Silent Night," and now, as she stood with the light of the hall sconces illuminating her in the doorway—under the mistletoe. She still wore the same gown, her curls were still piled high on her head, but now she was wrapped in a silver shawl, one that shimmered in the light of the candles.

"Shouldn't you be resting that ankle?" he asked, just as quietly.

She walked across the room, the slightest limp evident. Either she had not injured it as badly as he suspected, or she was a good actress, because he might not have noticed had he not been watching for it.

And he had been watching.

"I couldn't think of sleeping." She stopped before him and wrapped the shawl tighter around her shoulders.

"Too much on your mind?"

Her brown eyes were warm and inviting as she studied him. "Too much on my heart."

He wanted to ask her what she meant, but she turned her gaze to look out the window.

"I'm hopeless," she whispered, blowing her breath against the windowpane. A circle of fog formed on the glass and she made a star with her finger in the fading frost.

"Hopeless?"

"At flirting."

He finally found something to smile about again. "I hadn't noticed."

She gave him a look and said, "You're too kind."

"When have you known me to be kind?" he teased.

She tilted her head. "That's true." But the

teasing gleam in her eye faded and her shoulders sagged. "I'll never secure Lord Wessex's proposal before Christmas Eve if I can't flirt with him."

The thought of her engagement to Wessex made Christopher feel angrier than it should. "Nonsense." He shook his head, trying to push aside his ridiculous reaction to her words. "Wessex is well aware of you—and it's not because you flirt."

"He is?" She looked up surprised. "How do you know?"

Christopher rubbed the back of his neck, irritation at her naivete making him turn away from her to pace to the other window. "He watches your every move, he goes out of his way to assist you when necessary—and even when it's not. He barely tolerates the other men and he doesn't look twice at the other women." Now that he was far enough away, Christopher turned back to face her. "He'll make his intentions known sooner rather than later. Then you and I will be free of this agreement."

"Do you truly think so?" Her eyebrows lifted and her gaze filled with hope.

He couldn't bear to see it. "I don't know why he wouldn't."

"Why do you sound angry? Do you think I'm not worthy of Lord Wessex?"

"Ashleigh." He took a step toward her again, wanting her to know the truth. "*He's* not worthy of *you.*"

Silence filled the air as she studied him. "Do you jest?"

He shook his head, his face and voice as serious as they'd ever been. "I wish you could see yourself as the rest of us see you." He took another step toward her. "If you did, you would not settle for someone like Wessex. You deserve so much more."

A frown creased her delicate brow. "Lord Wessex is the most sought-after bachelor in England."

"Maybe you should look beyond England."

She didn't say anything for a moment, but then she whispered, "Where do you suggest I look?"

Everything in him wanted to suggest she look no farther than the man standing before her, but he had no right to make such a bold statement, nor did he truly believe he wanted her to. Nothing had changed since he'd left London two days ago. When he returned home, he'd be back at his demanding work, with no time for the finer things in life... namely a wife.

The conversation had become much too serious for him, and it had taken a turn he didn't expect. "I hear Belgium is a good place to look for a husband."

Instead of smile at his joke, she bristled at his words.

"Now, what's wrong with that?" he asked, trying to lighten the mood. "Don't you speak Dutch?"

She lifted her chin, just like he'd seen her do when she was a child. "You think it's funny that I'm trying to secure a husband?"

He'd embarrassed her, when all he'd meant to do was hide his own emotions. "That's not what I—"

"I don't think it's humorous at all." Her voice quivered, as if she might cry.

The very thought made Christopher panic. "It's not funny." He shook his head.

She took a step away from him and he wanted to reach out to stop her before she left angry.

"Before you arrived, I had no intention to seek a husband."

"I had nothing to do with that agreement."

"No, you didn't, but if you hadn't come, it would have been forgotten and I would not be in this predicament."

"My father was the one who—"

"You're a grown man. You could have refused."

He bristled at her words. "Just like you're refusing? I thought we both agreed that we'd follow through with the stipulations of the agreement in honor of our mothers."

She rubbed her hands up and down her arms. "Yes, well, I'm having second thoughts. I don't believe I can go through with this, after all. I have no hope with Lord Wessex, and I couldn't possibly marry you." She paused, her eyes softening with regret.

Her words stung more than they should, but he couldn't reveal as much to her. He knew he wasn't as desirable a match as Lord Wessex, but it burned, nonetheless.

"I'll do all in my power to see that Wessex has

every opportunity to make his intentions known so you're not obligated to do something as horrible as marry me." He took a step back and bowed. "Good night, Lady Ashleigh."

With that, he left the drawing room.

∞ ∞ ∞

Ashleigh stood by the cold window and watched Christopher leave. She wanted to call him back and explain that she hadn't meant to hurt his feelings. The more she had come to know him, the more she had found to admire. If he didn't live in America, she could almost see herself marrying a man like him—if she must.

When Christopher had hinted that she should look beyond England for a husband, she had half hoped he was referring to himself. But his joke about searching Belgium just confirmed that he was teasing her, and she had felt like a fool. He had made it clear that he wasn't interested in a wife, least of all her.

Yet, she couldn't deny that she had wanted him to be serious.

Suddenly, she felt far too tired to contemplate such things this evening. Her ankle was uncomfortable and she shouldn't be walking on it.

She left the drawing room and entered the large hall. The house was quiet and dark as she took her time going up the steps, her thoughts on

Christopher. His bedroom door clicked shut to her left when she came to stand at the stop of the stairs.

Part of her wanted to go to him and explain that she hadn't meant to be rude, but it wouldn't be proper to go to his room. She would have to seek out his company tomorrow—something she was finding less bothersome.

A noise in one of the alcoves caused her to pause on her way to her bedroom. Feminine giggles were followed by a man's deep voice.

Was someone having a tête-à-tête? If she continued, the couple would see her and know that she had heard them. If she stayed where she was, she took the risk of being an eavesdropper. It would be within her rights to confront these people, whoever they were, but did she want to? It would only embarrass everyone involved.

"Lord Wessex," the woman purred. "You are a rake!"

Ashleigh caught her breath. If she wasn't mistaken, it was the voice of one of her maid, Mary.

The woman left the alcove and entered the hall, adjusting her cap to sit properly on her brown curls. "The others will wonder why I'm not in my room," she said.

It was Mary!

"When will I see you again?" Eric left the alcove directly after her.

"We can meet here tomorrow evening when everyone is in bed." Mary's back was toward Ashleigh. She didn't see Ashleigh as she stood on

GABRIELLE MEYER

tiptoe and received another passionate kiss from Eric before rushing down the hall toward the servants' stairs.

Ashleigh was speechless as she watched the maid go. She would be forced to speak with her about the incident in the morning, but at the moment, she was more concerned about speaking to Eric.

He turned—and found Ashleigh staring. He didn't seem at all embarrassed to discover her standing there. "Ashleigh, what are you doing up so late?"

She wrapped her shawl around her shoulders by crossing her arms. "I should ask the same of you, Lord Wessex."

"I told you to call me Eric." He acted as if nothing untoward had just happened. "But what a happy coincidence that we're both awake. Now I can speak to you privately."

"Happy coincidence?" Was the man mad? "I just found you dallying with my maid, and you call it a happy coincidence?"

"That?" He waved down the hall with a shake of his head. "That didn't mean anything. Just a little bit of fun. Nothing serious."

Ashleigh's lips parted. "A little bit of fun? Have you no morals, sir?"

"Morals?" His voice was serious. "I have the same morals as everyone else. I attend church, pay my tithes, and see to the needs of those beneath me."

"Those are not the morals I was referencing."

She straightened her shoulders to reach her full height. "You are not married to that girl, nor do I suspect you intend to marry her."

He laughed. "Of course not. What does a midnight tryst have to do with marriage?"

Ashleigh moved back, hardly able to believe her ears. "I imagine it means a great deal to your future wife."

"Speaking of future wives." He came toward her, closing the distance between them, a charming smile on his face. "I've been meaning to speak to you about my intentions since I arrived."

"I no longer wish to know what those are." She began to move around him, but he put out his arm to stop her.

"I believe you do." He lowered his arm and studied her, much too close for her liking. "There are a hundred women who would marry me tomorrow, if I asked, but I've chosen you. I believe we would make a good match."

His statement would have been welcomed earlier, but now she wanted nothing to do with him. "You'd have more success if you asked one of the others."

"That's not possible."

"Why not?"

"Because you're the one I want."

His impertinence was beginning to annoy her. "Why?"

"You come from a good family, you'll have a substantial dowry, and you're beautiful." He touched her cheek with a feather-soft brush of his fingertips. "And I decided I would be the one to win your hand."

His words and actions matched what she knew of him. He was a flirt, a tease, and a rake, just as Mary said—though Mary seemed enamored with that idea and Ashleigh detested it.

Eric bowed and took a step back. "But this is not how I intended to propose. You are a lady and you should be courted and wooed."

"That won't be necessary."

He put his hand over his heart. "I insist. You'll see that I'm a good, honorable man, and I would make a superb husband."

"I—"

"Good night, Ashleigh." He walked away without waiting for her to respond.

He was the second man that evening who had left her feeling out of sorts, but for two very different reasons.

At least now she didn't need to worry about flirting with the arrogant Lord Wessex. As far as she was concerned, he was no longer a marriageable option.

But who would be? She couldn't imagine being married to any of the other men in her house party, and there wouldn't be time to find anyone else.

That left her with two options. Either go through with the agreement and marry Christopher, or deny her mother's wishes and forget the whole thing.

Neither seemed like a good idea.

But there was a third option, one she hadn't thought of before.

Ashleigh smiled into the dark hallway.

She would need to speak to Christopher first thing in the morning.

Chapter Five

The day before Christmas Eve was clear and bright. Ashleigh stood outside the library doors and braced herself to speak to Christopher. She had overheard her father telling Christopher about his immense collection of books, and Christopher had said he'd like to see it for himself right after breakfast.

Truth be told, she'd rather spend all day in the library as well, but hosting a houseful of people did not lend itself to her quiet ways.

She opened the library door and found Christopher sitting in an oversized chair, near one of the large windows, a red-covered book in hand. It was well-worn, and when she drew closer, she knew why. It was Charles Dickens's, *A Christmas Carol.* One of her favorite stories. Her father had given her a beautiful fiftieth-anniversary edition a few years back, but she still cherished the original copy she'd grown up reading. The one Christopher held in his hands.

He put his finger on a line in the book and

looked up to see who had entered. When he saw it was her, he set it aside and stood. "Ashleigh."

The reminder of how he'd left the night before, when she had insulted him, was still fresh between them this morning. The last thing she wanted was to hurt him, again, yet what she had come to suggest would not sit well between them either.

"I thought you'd be entertaining Wessex this morning," he said with little emotion.

Ashleigh had been able to avoid Eric, but only because Cynthia was near his side, hanging on his every word. Ashleigh would have to work hard to evade him for the remainder of his stay.

"That's one of the reasons I came to speak to you today." She motioned for him to return to his seat and she took the one opposite him.

"Wessex has proposed?" he asked once he was settled.

Ashleigh had been taught to sit tall in her chair, to keep her posture erect, but the furniture in the library was not meant for formality. Neither, did it seem, was her relationship with Christopher. She settled back in the chair and studied the man across from her. No longer did she think of him as the horrible, annoying boy he had been. The man before her was kind, sincere, intelligent—and utterly too handsome. She felt more comfortable with him than anyone she'd ever known, as if they'd been friends all their lives.

"I've decided I will not marry Wessex."

GABRIELLE MEYER

Ashleigh tried to make her statement as lighthearted and confident as she could muster.

Christopher set his elbows on the armrests and frowned. "Who will you marry then?"

She crossed her arms and lifted her chin. "No one."

His frown disappeared and he leaned forward. "What do you mean?"

"I'm not getting married. Not to Eric, not to you, not to anyone else."

"I don't understand."

It was her turn to lean forward. "Your mother is just as responsible for this mess as mine. Why should I be the one to marry a man I dislike, just so you can walk free?" She shook her head. "I refuse."

Christopher stood.

Ashleigh also stood. Though her head only came up to his shoulders, she tried to stare him down.

"I don't want to get married," he said. "I told you that the very first day I was here."

"I don't want to get married, either!"

"Even if I did," he went on, "I don't know anyone in England, besides you. I wouldn't have enough time to return to America and convince one of my acquaintances to marry me."

"Surely, you could convince someone." Her admiration colored the conviction in her voice. "A woman would be foolish not to accept your proposal."

The moment the words slipped out,

something shifted between them. It was evident in the way Christopher's shoulders relaxed and his face softened—and in the way her heart sped up and her mouth suddenly felt overly dry.

"What I mean," she said quickly, "is that you shouldn't have trouble finding a wife."

"By tomorrow?" He shook his head. "I'm not *that* desirable."

She wanted to disagree, but knew she'd only embarrass herself further. She said nothing, though she suspected the warmth in her cheeks revealed her thoughts.

"What happened with Wessex?" he asked.

She shuddered just hearing his name and walked over to the fireplace where she placed another log on the dying fire.

"Did he do something?" Christopher's American accent grew thicker as his anger surfaced.

"I have discovered some things about his character that convinced me I could not marry him."

"You shouldn't rely on gossip."

"It wasn't gossip." She repositioned the log with a poker and sent sparks dancing up the chimney. "I caught him in a compromising situation. When I confronted him, he acted as if nothing distasteful had occured. Then..." She paused, hating to recall how arrogant he was when he told her he planned to marry her. "He told me I would become his wife and wouldn't take no for an answer."

Christopher lifted his hand and rubbed the

back of his neck. "I've never liked him."

"That leaves me with no other options." She motioned to him. "So that's where you come in."

He paced across the library, kneading the muscles in his neck. Finally, he came to stop before her. "This is ridiculous, Ashleigh. We'll have to call the whole thing off. If my mother were here, and she understood the situation, I know she'd agree."

Ashleigh nibbled her bottom lip. Would her mother agree to call if off, as well? She wanted to believe that Mother would be understanding—but she couldn't be sure. Obviously, the agreement meant a great deal to both women, or they wouldn't have signed the documents.

But would they truly want Ashleigh and Christopher to get married, even if they didn't want to?

She couldn't imagine her mother wanting her to be unhappy.

But *would* she be unhappy married to Christopher?

"Maybe you're right," Ashleigh said slowly, watching his face to see how he felt about the possibility of being married to her.

"Then we agree?" There was so much hope in his voice. "We'll call off the agreement and be done with this nonsense?"

It was clear that he still wanted his freedom.

"Yes," she said.

He let out a relieved sigh and pulled her into his arms. "Thank you."

She froze in his unexpected embrace.

He released her just as quickly. "I'm sorry." He laughed uncomfortably. "I'm just so relieved."

Ashleigh tried not to let his words sear her heart. Of course he'd be relieved not to have to marry her. He didn't love her, he didn't want a wife, and he definitely didn't want to marry an English woman who wasn't familiar with his American ways.

She clasped her hands and turned away from him to look at the fire. "I-I suppose you will leave now."

He was quiet for a moment and then kicked an ember back into the fire. "I have been eager to return to London. There is a firm considering an investment in my railroad, and I'd like to be there for the vote."

They watched the fire crack and pop for another moment as her pulse slowed to a steady beat.

"It's my last hope for purchasing a section of railroad that's vital to our business," he said after a while.

"What will you do if they won't invest?"

He put his hands in his pockets, his countenance heavy. "I'll have to forget about expanding our railroad. Someone else will pick up the Northern Union soon."

"You want this very much, don't you?"

He turned his gaze away from the fire and she felt as if she was looking straight into his heart.

"More than anything. My father didn't have

the time of day for me as a child. The first time I recall him meeting my eye was when we were driving away from Anglesey Abbey after I had started that fire." He lifted a heavy shoulder. "But it wasn't pride or acceptance in his gaze. He was ashamed of me. After my mother died, it only became worse. He didn't start to pay attention to me until I showed an aptitude for the railroad business."

"Is that why you've given your entire life to your work?"

"I suppose it sounds ridiculous, but I guess it's true."

"And that's why this acquisition is so important? Because you want to make your father proud?"

He slowly nodded. "I hadn't thought about my motivation so deeply before now, but you're probably right." He readjusted one of the logs with his foot. "Does that make me sound pathetic?"

She shook her head and put her hand on his arm. "It makes you sound like a loving son."

Christopher rested his hand on top of hers. It sent warmth up her arm and into her chest.

"It sounds as if that Christmas so long ago affected both of us profoundly, for different reasons," she said softly. "After that day, my mother never asked me to perform a social obligation again. I embarrassed her deeply and made her ashamed of me."

He turned to face her, but didn't let go of her hand. Instead, he held it tighter. "How could your mother possibly be ashamed of you? You're beautiful, intelligent, humble, and the kindest woman I've ever met."

The warmth in her chest grew, until it filled every part of her. "You're too generous with your compliments." She couldn't help but tease. "Just like an American."

"I think you like it," he said with laughter in his voice. "I think you'd like a lot about America."

She loved the feel of his hand holding hers and didn't want him to let go. But she knew if she didn't pull away now, she might lose her heart to this handsome, kind American, and that would never do. Especially because he didn't want a wife.

Didn't want her.

"I imagine we won't see each other again," she said quietly as she pulled away from his hold.

He clasped his hands behind his back. "If you ever come to St. Paul, I hope you'll look me up."

She giggled, wanting to add levity to the moment. "I have never even considered visiting St. Paul, though your father speaks highly of Minnesota. I do admire Longfellow's 'Song of Hiawatha' and have always thought it would be romantic to see Minnehaha Falls."

"You and everyone else." He smiled.

"You must agree to come and see me next time you're in London."

He nodded, but didn't say anything.

A week ago, she couldn't imagine inviting Christopher Campbell to be her guest—but now, she couldn't imagine waiting eleven more years to see him again. The very thought made her want to cry.

"Will you write?" he asked quietly.

She suddenly felt shy and couldn't meet his eyes. "Would you like me to?"

"Very much."

"Then I will."

He reached out and took her hand again. "Ashleigh—"

"Campbell." Eric stood in the open door, his jaw tight. "I've been looking all over for you two. I thought I might find you together."

Ashleigh took her hand out of Christopher's, her heart beating hard. "Eric."

He strode into the room, his gaze burning into Christopher. "You've been summoned to London."

"By whom?" Christopher asked.

"A messenger just arrived from London. I took the note and said I'd deliver it to you personally." Eric stopped beside Ashleigh, but addressed Christopher as he handed him a piece of paper. "The messenger said they will be voting tomorrow morning and would like to meet with you this evening to discuss a few more details."

Christopher met Ashleigh's gaze. "I must go immediately."

"Of course."

"If they vote early enough in the day, I will return before your ball tomorrow evening." He smiled and the teasing gleam returned to his eye. "I know how much you want me to be at the tree lighting ceremony."

She had dreaded the ceremony every year since she was eight years old. Now, for the first time, she eagerly anticipated the event, knowing Christopher would be there with her. "More than you might know."

His smile faded and something far different shone from his face. Hope? Anticipation? Dare she think, affection? "Good-bye, Ashleigh."

"Good-bye, Christopher." She didn't want to be alone in the library with Eric, so she added, "I'll see you out."

He indicated for her to precede him out of the library and left her in the front hall while he went upstairs to pack a bag for the overnight jaunt to London.

"Now that Campbell is out of the way," Eric said as he joined Ashleigh, "maybe you'll pay more attention to me."

The very thought made her shiver.

∞ ∞ ∞

The following afternoon, Ashleigh stood inside the ballroom with Mrs. Rodgers, her housekeeper, going over the final preparations for the ball that evening. All around, the servants were busy moving potted plants, hanging pine boughs, stringing ornaments, and rearranging furniture.

"We will be expecting a hundred and fifty

guests?" Mrs. Rodgers asked for the tenth time that morning.

"Yes," Ashleigh said patiently.

"And you are sure you want to serve the buffet at ten o'clock? Isn't it popular to serve a midnight buffet?"

"I would like everything to be exactly the same as when my mother hosted the ball."

"Of course," Mrs. Rodgers said, her voice dry. "Just like we've always done."

"There's no reason to change." Ashleigh clasped her hands and took a deep breath, just as her mother would have done when dealing with a difficult servant. "Is there anything else we need to discuss?"

Mrs. Rodgers bowed her graying head. "I believe we have everything under control."

"Then I will see to my other guests." Some of the women were napping in preparation for the late-night festivities, while the men were in the drawing room passing the time playing whist or chess. Though Ashleigh longed to join the ladies, there was far too much to do before the dressing gong would sound later in the day. She still needed to meet with the cook to finalize the menu and the butler to discuss a few issues that had arisen with one of the footmen.

The hall clock chimed three times when she left the ballroom. Almost of their own accord, her feet took her to the front windows where she looked out at the long, empty drive.

Longing filled her chest with an ache she'd never felt before.

Was Christopher on his way back to her? It was a four-hour ride from London. If the firm had met early in the morning, he might arrive at any moment. Joy filled her with excitement at the thought of seeing him again. Had he been granted the money? Would he ask her to dance? Her ankle still smarted, but she could endure almost any pain to dance in his arms. Would he be shocked to know she had placed him beside her at the table? It was a spot reserved for the most honored guest at the party. She could think of no one else who was as special as him.

She might not be able to stop him from returning to America, but she'd enjoy every moment she possibly could with him before he left.

"There you are." Eric strode toward Ashleigh from the drawing room doors. "I've been trying to find you alone since yesterday."

She had successfully avoided him since their unfortunate encounter in the hallway two nights before. Why had she allowed herself to be alone now?

"I hate to be rude, but I have many things to attend to this afternoon." She started to pass him, but he stepped into her way. "I beg your pardon," she said with frustration in her voice. "Please let me pass.

He put his hands on her upper arms and held her in place. "I will not be dismissed, Ashleigh."

"Unhand me, Lord Wessex."

"Not until you agree to stay here and listen to me."

Heat climbed her neck and into her cheeks. If someone should happen upon them, they might think the worst, seeing her in his arms. "Fine."

"Good." He let her go. "I have something very important to discuss with you and I cannot abide chasing after anyone."

Except a lady's maid, she thought ruefully.

"What do you need to discuss with me?" she asked, knowing full well she would not agree to any proposition he might make.

"I would like to announce our engagement this evening at the ball."

"Our engagement?" Her face contorted in disgust. "I have not agreed to marry you."

"Is this about the American?"

"Christopher?"

"Do you fancy yourself in love with him?"

Love? The very thought made her heart quicken. Was she in love with Christopher? It seemed preposterous so soon after being reacquainted—yet, she couldn't deny her deep affection for him, or the sadness she felt when thinking about him leaving without her.

"You *are* in love with him." Eric's voice filled with incredulity and accusation. "I had suspected, but now I'm certain."

She didn't bother denying or confirming his claim. "It is none of your business."

"I disagree." His eyes were hard. "I have decided to make you my wife, so it is my business."

"I'm tired of this conversation, Lord Wessex."

"Then I will get right to my point." He straightened his posture and looked down his nose at her. "We will announce our engagement this evening, or I will advise my board to vote down Mr. Campbell's request for the funds."

She frowned. "What do you mean?"

"I am the principal financier for Thomas, Crenshaw & Hughes, the investment firm your American is asking to finance his railroad." His smile was triumphant. "Say the word, and I will tell my board to give him the money."

Sweat gathered on her palms and her heart beat an unsteady rhythm. "How long have you known?"

"I've always known. I simply chose not to mix business with pleasure. It didn't matter to me until now."

"If I marry you, you'll give him the money?"

"If you agree to marry me and announce it at the ball tonight, Campbell will get his money."

She put her hand to her throat, afraid to ask the next question. "And if I don't?"

"Then I will deny his request."

He said it with no feeling, though it stirred deep emotion in Ashleigh.

It would be within her power to grant Christopher what he wanted: his railroad, and ultimately, his father's respect.

What did she have to lose? She didn't love Eric, but she imagined he would provide well for her and she wouldn't be far from her father. If she had control over her own money, she would offer to give it to Christopher, but as it was, her father would never agree to finance something for the Campbells. His dislike of the elder Campbell was still strong, even more so with the boisterous man staying at Anglesey Abbey these past few days.

The only thing left to consider were her feelings for Christopher. Perhaps she did love him, but he had made it clear that he didn't want a wife. She couldn't hold out hope that he might propose to her someday. He would return to America soon and would probably never reappear. Even if he did, it might be years from now, and whatever feelings he might have for her would be cold by then.

"What will it be, Ashleigh?"

"You promise to give Christopher the money he's asked for?"

He placed his hand over his heart. "On my honor."

"Then I agree," she said quietly.

A look of conquest swept over Eric's face. "You won't regret this, my dear. Despite what you may think, I will be a good husband. In time, you'll come to love me."

Tears stung the back of Ashleigh's eyes as she nodded, hoping he was right, but fearing that she had just sealed her own fate.

Once the engagement was announced at the

ball, with over a hundred and fifty guests as witnesses, there would be no backing out of the agreement.

Chapter Six

The sun had already set as Christopher paced in the hallway outside the boardroom where he awaited the vote. What was taking so long? One delay after the other had kept them from meeting until after five o'clock. Didn't these men want to be home with their families for Christmas Eve festivities? Even if they voted now, he wouldn't make it back to Anglesey Abbey until after nine, and then he'd need to dress. If he was lucky, he might be there in time for the lighting of the Christmas tree right before the buffet.

He massaged the back of his neck as he walked the length of the hall, yet again. A carriage had been waiting for him for over two hours on the street outside. It would cost him a small fortune to pay the driver, but it would be worth it to see Ashleigh once again. He wanted to be there for the lighting of the tree, if for no other reason than to redeem his childhood mistakes.

The memory returned as if it were yesterday. As a child, Ashleigh had rescued many animals, but she had one cat in particular that she loved. It was a white, fluffy thing that her mother seemed to despise. Ashleigh carried it everywhere she went, so when it was time for the Christmas Eve ball, and it wasn't in her hands, Christopher had teased her about her cat not being invited to the party. She had stuck out her tongue and told him that the cat was in her room because it liked to climb trees, and her mother was afraid it would get into the Christmas tree.

That gave Christopher an idea.

Just before it was time to light the candles on the tree, he had snuck up to her room and lured the cat into his arms with a piece of smoked salmon from the kitchen. And when Ashleigh climbed the ladder to put the star on the top of the tree, he had let the cat go. He thought it would be funny to see the cat climb the tree, nothing more. He caught Ashleigh's eye the moment the cat leapt out of his arms, and she had scowled at him.

What happened next was branded into his memory for eternity. The cat made the tree start to wobble, which caused Ashleigh to lose her balance on the ladder. When the tree crashed to the ground, it looked as if it had been her fault.

The following hour was the most horrible one of his life. A nearby drape caught on fire, and the servant standing by with a wet sponge tried valiantly to put it out, but it was no use. Guests ran screaming from the room while the servants fought to get the fire under control.

The only people who witnessed what he had done were his parents. The very next day, they packed everything up and left for home, weeks earlier than planned. His mother had died on the way, leaving things unsettled with Ashleigh's mother.

It had been Christopher's fault, yet Ashleigh had taken the blame. She'd lived with the shame of it all these years. It was a wonder that she had welcomed him back to Anglesey Abbey—and that they had somehow found a friendship.

He paused as he looked out a window onto the bustling London street. A lamplighter walked on stilts, turning on the street lights as the evening sun faded. Snow had begun to fall, gathering quickly on the road, the lamps, and the buildings.

Were he and Ashleigh friends, or had they bypassed friendship all together? What he felt for her was more than friendly. Yesterday, in the library, he'd had the desire to bare his heart to her. He trusted her, admired her, and maybe, if he was honest with himself, he might even be in love with her. The thought of putting an ocean between them, and waiting for weeks on end to exchange letters, was a gloomy prospect.

"Mr. Campbell?" The door creaked open and the mustached Mr. Thomas motioned him inside the room. "We've come to a decision."

Casting aside thoughts of Ashleigh for the moment, Christopher followed him into the boardroom and faced the nine men who had control over his future.

"All of us would like to get home to our families, so we won't waste any more time." Mr. Thomas was a surprisingly young man, and he seemed a bit perturbed at the moment. "We've agreed to invest in your railroad, though it wasn't a unanimous decision."

Christopher's mouth parted at the news.

"You may come back after Christmas to sign all the legal documents before we have the money wired to your account." Mr. Thomas closed a folder and took his coat off the hook near the door. "I'm going home."

He left the room before Christopher could even thank him.

"If you'll excuse me," Christopher said to the other men around the table. "I'd like to thank all of you, starting with Mr. Thomas."

The others nodded as they stood to gather their things.

Christopher entered the hall again and sprinted to reach Mr. Thomas before he stepped outside.

"I'd like to thank you and wish you a Merry Christmas," he said.

"Don't thank me." Mr. Thomas put on his hat and tapped it firmly. "If I'd had my way, we wouldn't be giving you or any other American money to build your infrastructure."

Christopher wouldn't let Mr. Thomas's sour mood deter him or dampen his spirits. "Regardless,

I'd still like to thank you."

"Thank Lord Wessex, if you must thank someone."

"Lord Wessex?"

Mr. Thomas gave Christopher a shrewd look. "He's the one who advised everyone else to vote in your favor. He is a principal financier, and they would not go against his wishes."

Christopher frowned in confusion. "Why would Wessex want to finance my railroad?"

The investor studied Christopher, as if trying to decide whether or not to divulge information. "Since I don't care for Wessex, then I'll tell you what I heard, though I don't put much stock in rumors."

"What did you hear?"

"Apparently, he wants to marry Lady Ashleigh Arrington and this investment is somehow wrapped up in his personal problems." Mr. Thomas leaned forward as he pulled on his gloves. "She agreed to marry Wessex if he gave you the money. They'll announce their engagement this evening at Anglesey Abbey."

It felt as if a steel fist punched Christopher in the gut and he could only stare at the other gentleman.

"I don't know how you're involved in the affair," Mr. Thomas said, "but I imagine you used the lady to your advantage. Congratulations." With that, he left the building.

Christopher stared after the man as the door slammed shut.

Ashleigh agreed to marry Wessex if he'd give Christopher the money? What kind of a man would ask her to do such a thing?

And how much did Ashleigh care for Christopher to agree?

Anger burned in his gut as he pushed open the door and rushed into the street. Snow continued to fall, casting a thick blanket over the dirty city.

He couldn't let Ashleigh go through with it. There wasn't anything he wanted more than her happiness. Not a railroad, not his father's acceptance, and definitely not Lord Wessex's money. If he didn't get to Anglesey Abbey before the announcement was made, it would be too late. She'd be as good as married in the eyes of the peerage.

"Take me to Anglesey Abbey in Cambridgeshire, posthaste," he called out to the driver as he jumped into the carriage.

The next four hours would be the longest of his life. He had to get to Ashleigh before she made an announcement. Not only to stop her from agreeing to marry Wessex, but to tell her what he'd come to realize while he'd been away.

He loved her and he didn't want her to marry anyone, but him.

∞ ∞ ∞

"Ashleigh?" Father spoke her name quietly, a question in his tone.

She turned away from the window where she had been watching the snow fall. The orchestra played a beautiful waltz in the ballroom, just down the hall. She should have been mingling with her guests, playing the part of hostess, but she didn't have the heart.

The ballgown she wore was the most beautiful dress she had ever owned. Dark green silk, just off the shoulders, with a slight train. She had hoped Christopher would return in time to see her in it—but now none of that mattered.

Father's eyes were sad as he smiled at her. "Are you ready?"

It was almost time to light the candles on the Christmas tree and make her announcement. Eric had hardly left her side all evening, until she insisted she needed a moment alone. But she hadn't been able to bring herself to return to the ballroom and into his keeping.

She let out a sigh and linked her arm through her father's. "I suppose I can't put it off forever."

"Why are you doing this?" He put his hand over hers. "Why are you marrying Wessex when you don't want to?"

She hadn't shared the truth with her father. Knowing him, he'd put a stop to such a thing—yet, he wouldn't give Christopher the money he needed, either. Ashleigh couldn't allow that to happen.

"I need to marry someone. Eric is just as good as the next man." She tried to smile, to reassure him, but her lips quivered and tears threatened.

"If this is about that agreement with the Campbells—" His voice became angry. "I will insist we forget about the whole ordeal. If they want to take us to court over the thing, I'll—"

"It's not about the agreement." She shook her head sadly. "It's not that at all." If it was as simple as that, she might have a bit of hope.

"Then what is it?"

She squeezed his arm and lifted her head. "It's nothing, Father. Let's go light those candles."

"Only if you're sure."

Ashleigh nodded. "I'm sure."

He leaned over and kissed her cheek. "If you're happy, I'm happy."

Happiness was not an option for Ashleigh right now, but she would do all she could to make the most of this situation. She knew dozens of women who were married to men out of convenience. Love wasn't the rule. It was the exception in most marriages. Who was she to expect anything more?

Yet, she couldn't stop thinking about Christopher. If she'd been forced to marry him, she knew she would love him, even if he never returned the love. He was a good man, one she would be honored to marry.

"I'm proud of you, Ashleigh. You've done a beautiful job stepping in as mistress of Anglesey Abbey."

His words made her heart glow, despite the troubles she faced. "Would Mother be pleased?"

"More than I could say."

Ashleigh sighed and dropped her gaze, but her father lifted her chin with his finger. "What's wrong?"

"I just wish I could have pleased her while she was alive."

He shook his head. "You pleased your mother a great deal. She couldn't have been happier with you."

It seemed a preposterous thought. "Then why did she never ask me to put the star on the top of the tree after that horrible Christmas? Why did she not ask me to perform other social obligations?"

Father laid his hand on her cheek and looked deep into her eyes. "She knew how you detested being the center of attention, so she decided not to make you uncomfortable again. She admired your self-confidence and independence. Your mother accepted you as you were. It was her gift to you."

Memories flooded Ashleigh's mind of times when her mother had let her be, instead of demanding that she fulfill all the social obligations other young women performed. Not once had Ashleigh thought it was because her mother understood her.

"Come," Father said. "And be the woman God made you to be." He led her out of the drawing room and into the hall. "And give Wessex a chance to prove himself. He might surprise you."

She nodded and smiled, just for him. "I will."

"That's a good girl." He rubbed the top of

her hand as they walked down the hall toward the ballroom.

The Christmas tree was set up in the parlor off the ballroom, as always. The servants had spent all day decorating it with family ornaments, colorful beads, and shiny tinsel. Just before the doors would open, they would light each of the candles, then Father would wish everyone a Merry Christmas and announce the engagement.

There would be no turning back after that. The very thought made her stomach sour.

They entered the ballroom and she greeted several guests as they walked to the parlor doors. By every account, the Christmas Eve party was a success. Everyone was laughing, dancing, and having a grand time. Candles dripped with wax, couples kissed beneath the mistletoe, and the smell of fresh pine garland filled her nose.

If only Christopher could be with her now to enjoy the festivities. His father stood on the opposite side of the room, laughing and making merry with the rest of the guests. Would Christopher be just as jolly this evening? By now, he would have learned about the investment. No doubt he was already making plans for his railroad. Just thinking about how happy he'd be took the edge off Ashleigh's melancholy.

"It's time." Father nodded to Mr. Warren, who signaled the orchestra to stop playing.

The dancers came to a halt and Mr. Warren rang a bell to get their attention.

Eric and his mother joined Father and Ashleigh as they stood outside the doors to the adjoining drawing room.

"I hope you know what you're doing, son," Eric's mother said under her breath.

Ashleigh pretended not to hear her and forced herself to smile at her guests.

"If you'll join us," Father addressed the crowd, "we'd like to usher in this blessed holiday with the lighting of our Christmas tree."

Two matching footmen opened the doors, allowing Ashleigh and her father to lead the way. Eric and his mother trailed close behind, followed by the rest of the guests.

Appreciative whispers filled the drawing room as people crowded in to see the magnificent tree. It stood fifteen feet tall and was aglow with candlelight.

If her own heart wasn't so heavy, she would enjoy reveling in the beauty of the moment.

At the top of the tree was a star, which had been placed there by a servant. Since that fateful Christmas, when Christopher had almost burned their house down, there was no special ceremony to put the star on top. It was done quietly and safely, away from the eyes of the guests.

Father squeezed her hand and stepped forward to address their guests.

"Thank you all for sharing this Christmas Eve with Ashleigh and me."

A commotion at the back of the crowded room

drew Ashleigh's attention. People began to move to the side, some with frowns, and others with exclamations of surprise.

"We both feel Elizabeth's presence," Father continued. "It is a great comfort to know that so many of you carry her memory in your hearts, especially at this time of year."

Ashleigh tried to concentrate on what he was saying, knowing that the most important part of his address would come at the end, but there was someone pushing their way to the front of the room. She couldn't make out who it was, but they were not stopping. Was someone that desperate to see the tree up close?

"On behalf of our family." Father reached out and took Ashleigh's hand. "I want to wish you a Merry Christmas."

The others wished her and Father a Merry Christmas in return.

Suddenly, Christopher appeared on the edge of the crowd. He wore an afternoon suit and his hair was disheveled as he searched the front of the room with anxious eyes, until his gaze landed on Ashleigh.

Her heart leapt and she almost took a step forward, but her father still held her hand.

"And speaking of family," Father continued, apparently unaware of Christopher's strange and sudden appearance, "I have a happy announcement to make."

Eric reached out and possessively took Ashleigh's other hand, his attention on Christopher.

The guests watched with open curiosity and avid interest. Cynthia, who had not been told about the engagement, blinked with surprise.

Christopher questioned Ashleigh with his eyes as he shook his head.

What was he doing? Ashleigh wanted to speak to him, but there was no way to step away from Eric now.

Father continued speaking. "It is with great pride that I—"

Christopher's eyes filled with panic and he took a step forward.

Ashleigh opened her mouth to stop her father, but everything was happening so quickly.

"—would like to announce the engagement of —"

A scream filled the air as a flame licked up the Christmas tree.

Father's announcement was lost in the chaos that erupted as several servants rushed to the tree to put out the fire. More people screamed as guests began to run out of the drawing room and into the ballroom. Smoke stung Ashleigh's nose as she pulled her hands away from her father and Eric.

She lost sight of Christopher as people pushed and shoved.

"Ashleigh." Suddenly, he was beside her, his hand on her elbow. He led her out of the parlor and through a door that connected with the library.

She went willingly and gratefully, coughing from the smoke. A glance over her shoulder revealed that the servants had the fire under control, and were calming the guests.

When she and Christopher were safely inside the library, he closed the door, and without a word, pulled her into his arms.

"Am I too late?" he whispered into her hair.

"Too late?" She was breathless as she clung to him.

"Did you and Wessex make the announcement?" He pulled back and placed his thumbs on her cheeks, gently brushing away the tears that she didn't know she had shed.

"No."

Christopher leaned his forehead against hers, breathing just as hard as her. "Thank God."

"How did you know?"

"One of the investors told me." He shook his head and pulled back, confusion on his handsome face. "Ashleigh, why would you marry Wessex for my sake?"

More tears stung the back of her eyes and her lips trembled. "If I don't marry him, you won't get the money you need for your railroad."

"I don't want Wessex's money." Pain filled his voice. "Especially if it means you'd have to marry him. I would give up everything for your happiness."

"Do you truly mean that?"

In answer, he pulled her closer and lowered his lips to hers.

His kiss was exquisite as his strong arms wrapped around her. His passion was matched only by his tenderness, and it was clear, by the way he held her, that he regarded her with deep affection. But his touch was tentative—until she lifted her hands to his face and returned his passion with her own.

He tightened his hold, deepening the kiss.

After a moment, he broke away, a surprised laugh on his lips. "I had no idea how you felt."

She smiled, loving the way his blue eyes sparkled with joy. "I didn't know how you felt either."

He kissed her again, erasing every last shred of doubt she might have.

"I still don't know why you would make such a sacrifice for me." He caressed her cheek with his thumb and she leaned into the touch.

"Because I love you," she said, watching the way her words changed the emotion on his face from happiness to wonder.

"I love you, too, Lady Ashleigh," he said softly. "I had no idea it could be possible in such a short time."

She could do nothing but smile, content to stay in his arms all evening.

"I suppose we must face everyone sooner or later," he finally said.

She took a deep breath and nodded. "There's the matter of Wessex—and the fire—to deal with." She paused. "Did you start the fire?"

He shook his head and laughed. "No, but I would have if your maid hadn't set the candle to the tree first."

"My maid?" She searched her memory. Who was standing beside the tree when she'd come into the drawing room? Her eyes opened wide. "Mary?"

"I don't know her name."

It *was* Mary. Had she been jealous? Ashleigh beamed. Whatever her reason, Ashleigh was thankful for what she'd done.

"So." Christopher crossed his arms, a mock frown upon his handsome face. "Your maid may start the tree on fire, and you are overjoyed, but if I do, you hold it against me for eleven years?"

Ashleigh laughed and placed a kiss on his cheek. "Maybe we should have electricity installed and use electric lights next year."

Christopher's mood suddenly grew serious. "Where will we be next Christmas?"

The simple question begged another. "Where would you like to be next Christmas?"

"Wherever you are."

Ashleigh's smile began slowly, but it blossomed, until it radiated from her heart. "Say the words and I will follow you anywhere."

He wrapped her in his arms again and pulled her close. "Will you marry me and go home with me to St. Paul?"

She had never, in her wildest imaginings, thought she'd marry an American and make her home in Minnesota. But she realized something standing there with Christopher. She would never be at home, unless she was by his side.

"I will."

Chapter Seven

The house was quiet as Ashleigh and Christopher met at the top of the stairs just as the sun filled the hall with the first hint of sunshine. Christmas morning was clear, crisp, and filled with a hint of smoke.

"Good morning," Ashleigh whispered, feeling a little shy in his presence during the light of day.

"Good morning." He reached out and offered his hand, which she took without hesitation.

"Did you sleep?" she asked quietly.

"No. You?"

"Not a wink." She smiled, feeling refreshed, despite her lack of rest.

"Are you ready?" he asked.

In answer, she led the way down the steps. The previous evening, she had told Eric that she would not be marrying him after all. When he'd threatened to rescind his offer to finance Christopher's railroad, she had said it didn't matter. Christopher wouldn't accept his money. Eric had left the house with his mother before the party ended.

Who knew what Lady Wessex would say to the London papers about her party now?

Ashleigh no longer cared, because now it was time to face their fathers.

They held hands as they walked to the morning room where her father would be eating breakfast and reading the morning paper.

Christopher had asked his father to meet them there at sunrise as well.

"No matter what is said..." Christopher held her back for a moment. "Know that I love you and I'll fight for you, if need be."

She placed her hand on his dear cheek and shook her head. "We can fight together." She started to open the door, but paused. "If it comes to that."

He grinned, but she saw the worry behind his eyes.

Truth be told, she didn't feel as confident as she'd like. If her father refused to let her marry Christopher, she could not dishonor him.

They entered the room, hand in hand, and found their fathers sitting at a table in the oriel window overlooking the gardens, now draped in a layer of fresh white snow.

Father's eyes immediately went to their clasped hands and then he looked up in surprise.

Mr. Campbell was reading a newspaper, but he, too, showed surprise at their entrance.

"Ashleigh?" Father stood and waited for them to cross the room.

"I've come to share some news with you," she

said with a trembling smile.

To his credit, Mr. Campbell didn't speak. Instead, he beamed.

"Lord Pemberton." Christopher addressed her father. "I would like to ask for your daughter's hand in marriage."

"I'm speechless." Father searched Ashleigh's face. "When did this happen?"

"I suppose it happened right away," she said. "But we weren't completely sure until last evening, during the fire."

"I love Ashleigh," Christopher said to her father. "And if you'll allow me, I'd like to marry her and take her to St. Paul."

"America?" Father didn't even look at Christopher. Instead, he continued to watch her. "Is this what you want?"

She held Christopher's hand in both of hers and nodded. "With all my heart."

For a moment, Father was quiet, but then he reached out for her.

Ashleigh left Christopher's side and entered her father's warm embrace.

"Then I will give you my blessing," he said as he hugged her. "I told you that if you're happy, I'm happy, and I meant it."

Ashleigh hugged him tighter. "Thank you."

"Congratulations," Mr. Campbell said to Christopher as he extended his hand. "I'm very happy for you."

"Thank you, Father." Christopher shook his

father's hand.

"Welcome to the family," Mr. Campbell said to Ashleigh. "I know my wife would be overjoyed, if she were still with us."

"I'm sure both of our wives would be overjoyed," Father said with certainty. "It's what they wanted from early on."

Christopher captured Ashleigh's hand in his.

She returned to his side, not wanting to leave it again.

"I was made aware of the situation with Lord Wessex last night," Father said, his face serious. "And I'm disappointed that you didn't let me know what was happening, Ashleigh."

Embarrassment warmed her cheeks, but she didn't respond.

"If you wanted to help Christopher finance his railroad, then you should have come to me."

Her mouth parted in surprise. "I didn't think you'd be interested."

"You never asked."

Ashleigh squeezed Christopher's hand.

"As a wedding gift to you both," Father said, putting his hand on Christopher's shoulder, "I would like to help. I have a few friends who have been interested in investing in American railroads, but have not had the ability to do it alone. I will gather them together and we will provide whatever you need."

"I would be honored to work with you, Lord Pemberton." Christopher reached out and shook

Father's hand. "Thank you."

Father put his other hand on Ashleigh's shoulder and smiled at both of them. "Just take care of my daughter and we'll both be happy."

"It will be my greatest privilege," Christopher said.

"And I will do my best to take care of your son," Ashleigh said with a smile at Mr. Campbell.

Father stepped back and Christopher put his arm around Ashleigh's waist, smiling down at her. "I think we'll do a fine job taking care of each other."

Ashleigh returned his smile and marveled that she had fallen in love with Christopher Campbell.

The child she disliked most in the world had somehow become the man she adored more than any other. And, for the first time since his arrival, she was thankful their mothers had made that Christmas promise so long ago.

About The Author

Gabrielle Meyer

Gabrielle Meyer lives in Minnesota on the banks of the Mississippi River with her husband and four children. As an employee of the Minnesota Historical Society, she fell in love with the rich history of her state and enjoys writing fictional stories inspired by real people, places, and events. You can learn more about Gabrielle and sign up for her newsletter at www.gabriellemeyer.com.

Instagram.com/gabrielle_meyer/
Facebook.com/AuthorGabrielleMeyer

Praise For Author

"With rich historical details and a riveting conundrum, When the Day Comes had me glued to the pages, the story tugging at my heart, and lingering with me long after the last page. A triumph of a story!"

—Susan May Warren, USA Today best-selling author of Sunrise

"Gabrielle Meyer's When the Day Comes is very intriguing—such a fresh, creative premise! The drama builds with each page and I could not wait to see how it would all turn out. Fans of history, romance, or time travel will adore this book."

—Julie Klassen, Bestselling Author

Books By This Author

When The Day Comes

Libby has been given a powerful gift: to live one life in 1774 Colonial Williamsburg and the other in 1914 Gilded Age New York City. When she falls asleep in one life, she wakes up in the other. While she's the same person at her core in both times, she's leading two vastly different lives.

But Libby knows she's not destined to live two lives forever. On her twenty-first birthday, she must choose one path and forfeit the other--but how can she choose when she has so much to lose in each life?

The Soldier's Baby Promise

Resolved to keep his promise, Lieutenant Nate Marshall returns home to look after the widow of his best friend, who was killed in the line of duty. Grieving mom Adley Wilson is overwhelmed by her bee farm, her grandfather-in-law who lives with her and her new baby. But accepting Nate's help may just be the lifeline she needs…

The Baby Proposal

Drew Keelan is the last person Whitney Emmerson imagined would propose to her. But when their infant nephew is orphaned and the will stipulates that to adopt him they must be married, Whitney and Drew have no choice. It's one thing to wed for custody, but do they have what it takes to make a marriage of convenience last till death do them part?

Snowed In For Christmas

Ending up snowbound with her ex for Christmas is a shock for Liv Butler—especially when she learns Zane Harris secretly adopted their child. While Liv longs to know the daughter she was forced to give up as a teen, Zane's girls are his priority, and the widower doesn't trust Liv to stay after the snow clears. But could she be just what his family needs?

Made in the USA
Columbia, SC
01 October 2022